The SOUND That JAZZ MAKES

by CAROLE BOSTON WEATHERFORD

illustrated by ERIC VELASQUEZ

Marshall Cavendish Children

This is Africa where rhythm abounds
and music springs from nature sounds,
played on a drum carved from a tree
that grew in a forest of ebony.

This is a kalimba chiming for rain
while a high priest chants the same refrain.
These are the dancers who leap and spin
wearing grass skirts and leopard skin.

This is the pulse of countless hearts
aboard the slave ships chased by sharks;
captives bound for a place unknown
on angry waves in boats that moan.

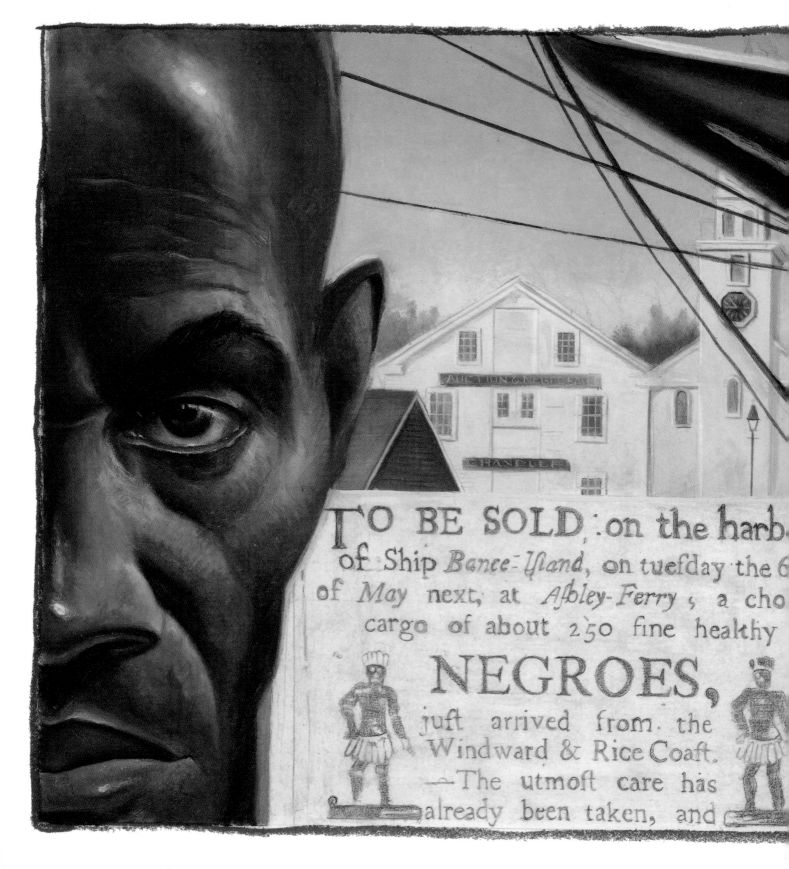

This is the harbor where slave ships docked
and Africans stood on auction blocks;
human chattel, bought and sold,
traded as if they were silk or gold.

AUCTION

This is the field where slaves turned the soil,
and chanted of freedom while they toiled
to pass the message, through secret codes,
of stealing away on pitch-dark roads.

This is how runaways asked the Lord
to guide them with the drinking gourd,
a compass in the sky at night
leading them onward in their flight.

This is the banjo the farmer plucked
after the corn was picked and shucked
while a young boy clacked a pair of spoons
and folks danced jigs beneath the moon.

These are cakewalkers dressed so fine
bouncing—hop-skip—down the line
to the steady beat of a ragtime tune
filling a honky-tonk saloon.

These are the songs of blood and sweat
of men laying tracks and casting nets,
of the Delta bluesman whose guitar whines,
who howls of heartbreak and hard times.

This is the church where gospel rocked,
with shouts of praise that called the flock
to lift their voices, clap their hands,
and march on toward the Promised Land.

This is the steamboat *Dixie Queen*
that showcased a combo from New Orleans,
where Satchmo learned to blow his horn
and some folks claim that jazz was born.

This is Harlem where Duke was king,
Lady was crowned, and Count ruled swing,
Cab Calloway hollered, "Hi-de-ho!"
and Ella scatted in the spotlight's glow.

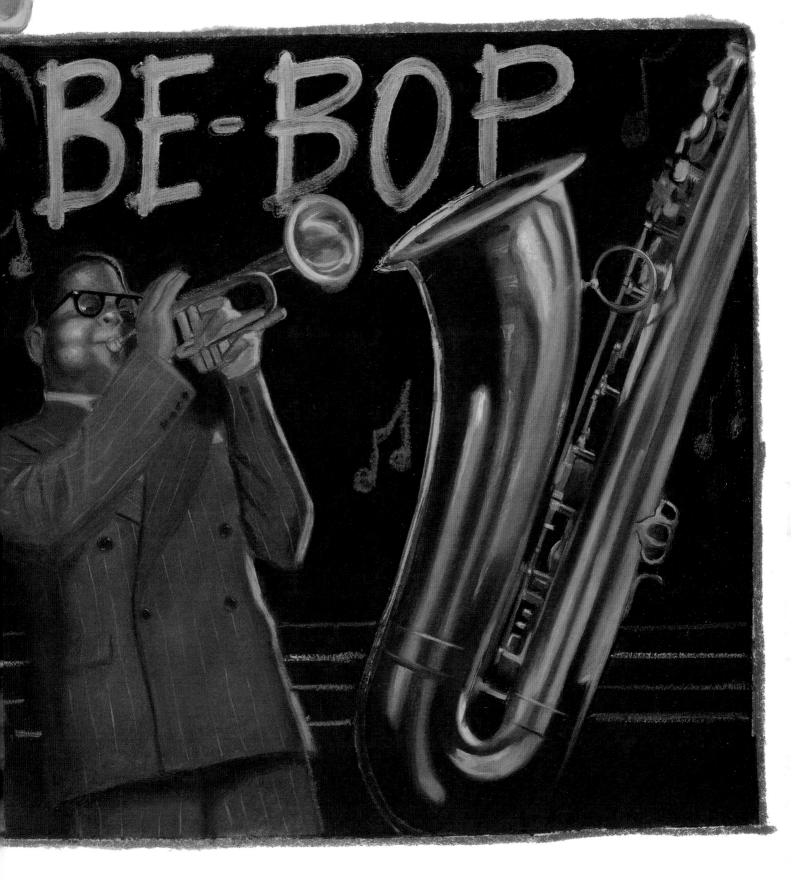

This is Birdland where jazz broke free
and the sounds of bebop came to be,
where horn men trumpeted things to come
and gold-toned saxophones blared and hummed.

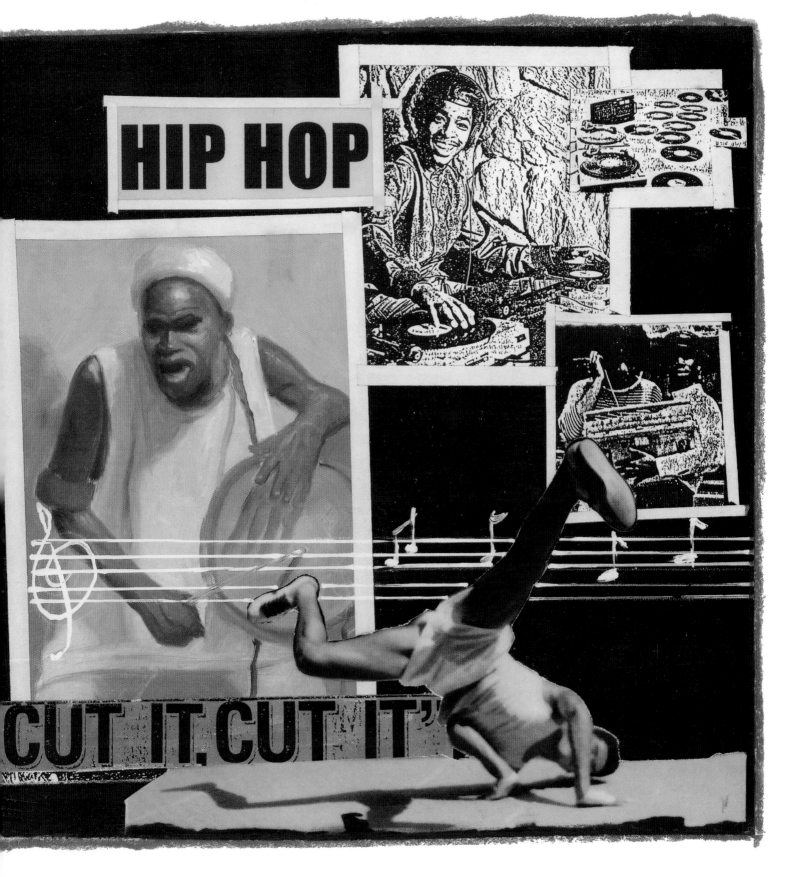

This is the rapper whose boom box blasts.
These are musicians inspired by the past.
They all hear the age-old, far-off beat
of Africa drumming on every street.

JAZZ is a downbeat born in our nation,
chords of struggle and jubilation,
bursting forth from hearts set free
in notes that echo history.

**This is
the sound
that jazz
makes!**

In memory of my father, who had an ear for good jazz. —C.B.W.
For the countless jazz musicians who have enriched our lives with their music. —E.V.

The paintings of Ella Fitzgerald, Cab Calloway, Billie Holiday, Count Basie,
and Duke Ellington are based on photographs taken by William Gottlieb.
The painting of John Coltrane is based on a photograph by Henri Dauman.

kalimba (kə-lĭm′bə)
n. An African musical instrument in the shape of a wooden box
set with metal bars that are plucked with the fingers.

Text copyright © 2000 by Carole Boston Weatherford
Illustrations copyright © 2000 by Eric Velasquez
First published in 2000 by Walker Publishing Company, Inc. (USA) and Fitzhenry and Whiteside (Canada)
First Marshall Cavendish paperback edition, 2010

Marshall Cavendish Corporation
99 White Plains Road
Tarrytown, NY 10591
www.marshallcavendish.us/kids

Library of Congress Cataloging-in-Publication Data
Weatherford, Carole Boston, 1956–
The sound that jazz makes / Carole Boston Weatherford ; Eric Velasquez. —
1st Marshall Cavendish paperback ed.
p. cm.
Originally published: New York : Walker & Co., 2000.
ISBN 978-0-7614-5732-9
1. Jazz—History and criticism—Juvenile literature. I. Velasquez, Eric, ill. II. Title.
ML3506.W42 2010
781.6509—dc22
2009029643

Editor: Robin Benjamin
Printed in Malaysia (T)

10 9 8 7 6 5 4 3 2 1